I'm Not Millie!

Mark Pett

Alfred A. Knopf   New York

THIS IS A BORZOI BOOK PUBLISHED BY ALFRED A. KNOPF

Copyright © 2019 by Mark Pett

All rights reserved. Published in the United States by Alfred A. Knopf,
an imprint of Random House Children's Books, a division of Penguin Random House LLC, New York.

Knopf, Borzoi Books, and the colophon are registered trademarks of Penguin Random House LLC.

Visit us on the Web! rhcbooks.com

Educators and librarians, for a variety of teaching tools, visit us at RHTeachersLibrarians.com

Library of Congress Cataloging-in-Publication Data
Names: Pett, Mark, author.
Title: I'm not Millie / Mark Pett.
Other titles: I am not Millie
Description: First edition. | New York : Alfred A. Knopf, [2019] | Summary: Someone is causing
a lot of trouble during and after supper, but Millie is certainly not the guilty one.
Identifiers: LCCN 2018008092 (print) | LCCN 2018015702 (ebook) | ISBN 978-1-101-93793-8 (trade) |
ISBN 978-1-101-93794-5 (lib. bdg.) | ISBN 978-1-101-93795-2 (ebook)
Subjects: | CYAC: Behavior—Fiction. | Identity—Fiction. | Humorous stories.
Classification: LCC PZ7.P4478 (ebook) | LCC PZ7.P4478 Iam 2019 (print) |
DDC [E]—dc23
The text of this book is set in 44-point Clarendon and 36-point Colby Narrow.
The illustrations were created using India ink and watercolor.

MANUFACTURED IN CHINA

November 2019
10 9 8 7 6 5 4 3 2 1
First Edition

For Millie

I'm afraid you're mistaken. I don't know who this Millie person is.

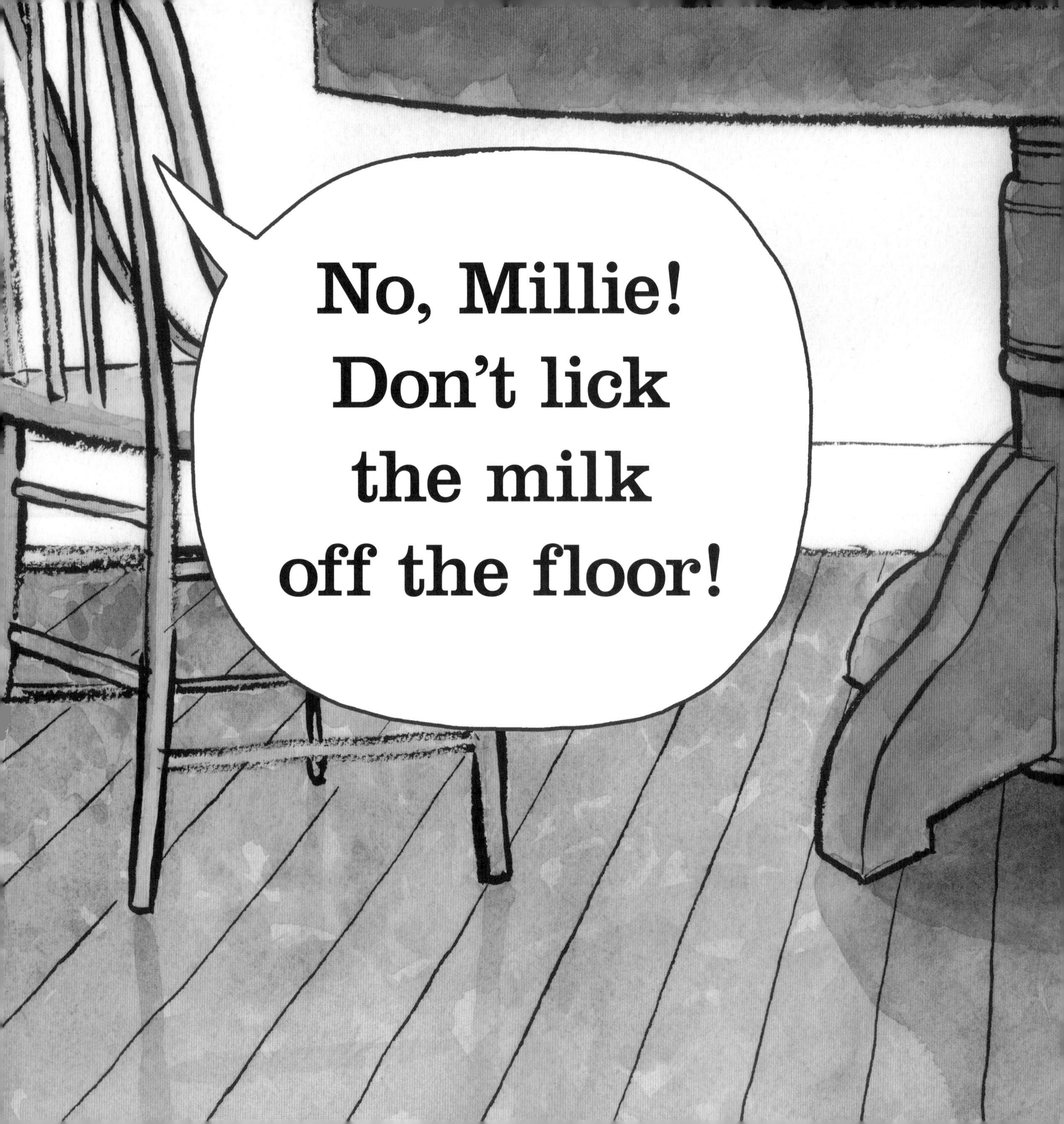
No, Millie! Don’t lick the milk off the floor!

Millie, you're making the lamp shake. Please stop jumping around the house.

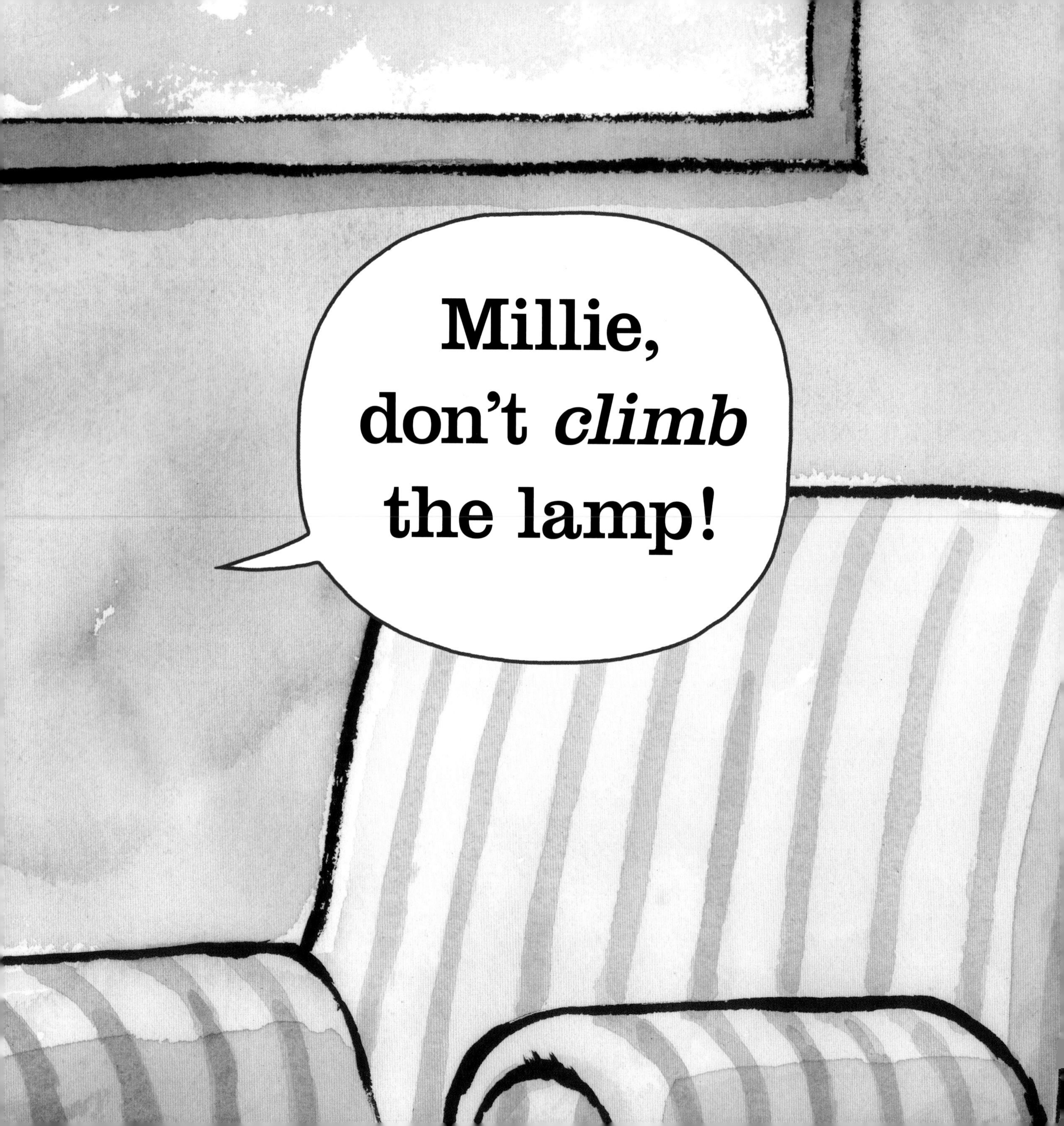
Millie, don't *climb* the lamp!

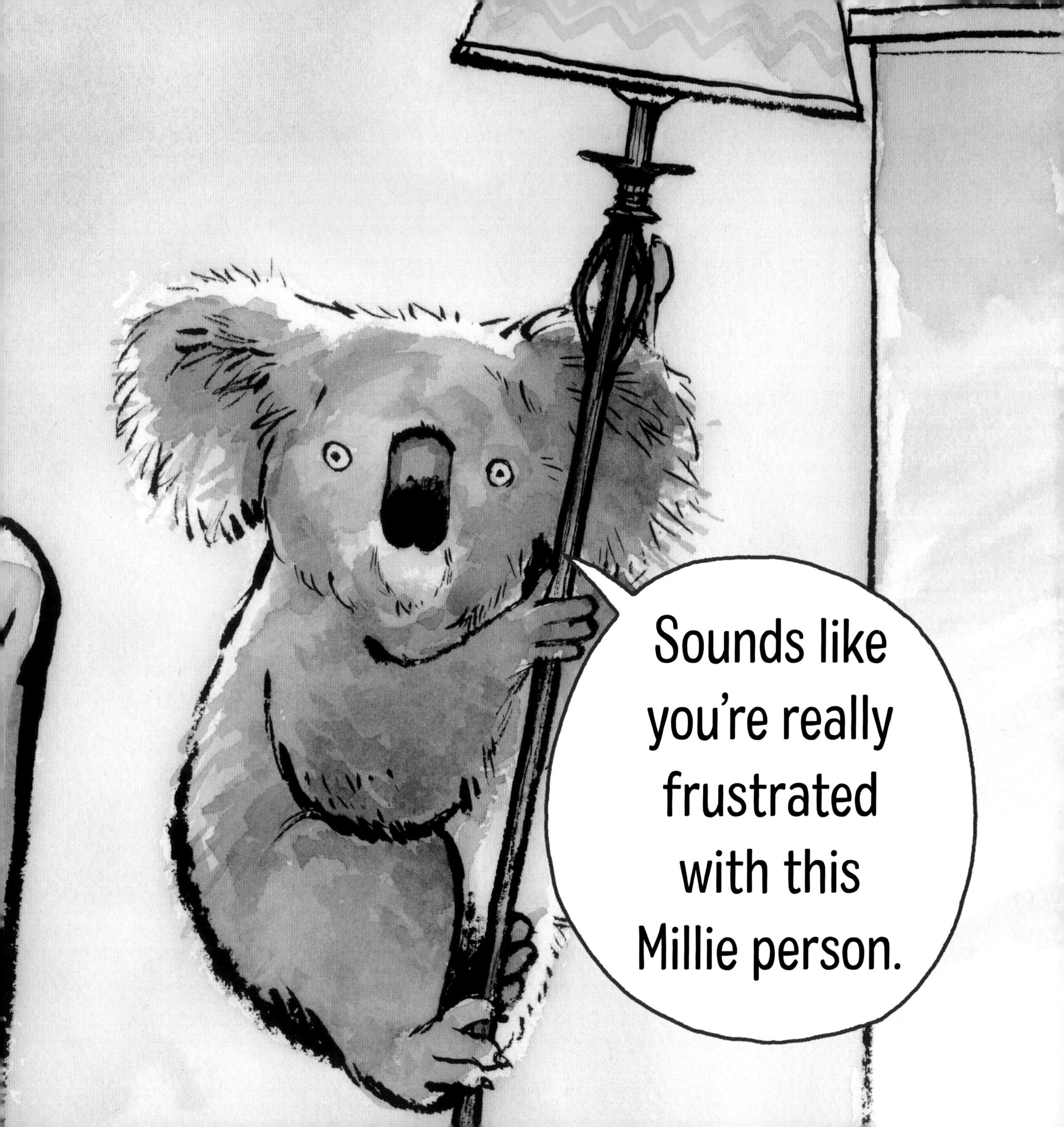

That's enough. It's time to get ready for your bath, Millie.

Oh, okay. Well, if you happen to *see* Millie, tell her I have some bubble-gum ice cream for her.